The Friend

John Burningham

CANDLEWICK PRESS
CAMBRIDGE, MASSACHUSETTS

Arthur is
my friend.

We always
play together.

We play outside
when it is nice,

and stay
inside when
it is raining.

Sometimes
I don't like
Arthur,

so Arthur
goes home.

Then I'm
by myself.

I have
other friends,
of course.

But Arthur
is my
best friend.

Second U.S. edition 1994
First published in Great Britain in 1975
by Jonathan Cape Ltd., London.

Library of Congress Cataloging-in-Publication Data

Burningham, John.
The friend / John Burningham.— 2nd U.S. ed.
Summary: Easy-to-read text and drawings describe a young boy's
relationship with his best friend Arthur.
ISBN 1-56402-327-3 (lib. bdg.)
[1. Friendship—Fiction.]   I. Title.
[PZ7.B936Fr   1994]
[E]—dc20   93-10331

10 9 8 7 6 5 4 3 2 1

Printed in Hong Kong

The pictures in this book were done in pastels, crayon, and ink.

Candlewick Press
2067 Massachusetts Avenue
Cambridge, Massachusetts 02140